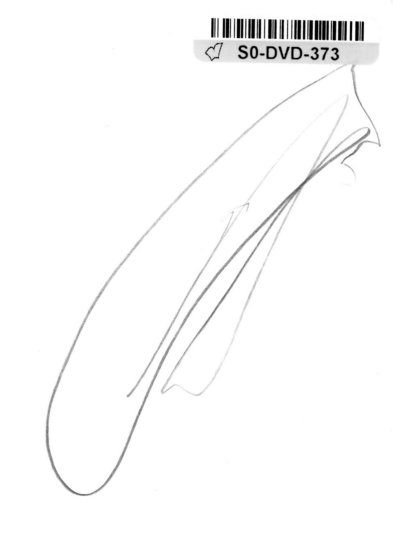

Fancy Dance in Feather Town

By Ann M. Martin
Illustrated by Henry Martin

For our own mother hens, Adele and Edie

A GOLDEN BOOK • NEW YORK
Western Publishing Company, Inc., Racine, Wisconsin 53404

On Monday Fran ran into Emma near the supermarket.

"How nice you look, Emma," said Fran.

"Why, thank you," said Emma. "I went to the feather-dresser. I'm going to the chicken dance on Friday."

"The chicken dance?" said Fran. "I'm going, too."

The chicken dance was the biggest event in Feather Town. Everybody went. And everybody got dressed up.

Fran looked at Emma. Emma looked nice. She looked very nice.
"Which feather-dresser did you go to?" she asked Emma.

"Paul's House of Feathers," replied Emma.

"Well, I have to go now," said Fran. "I'll see you later."

"'Bye," said Emma.

Fran ran down the street, straight to Paul's House of Feathers.

"Please, Paul," said Fran, "will you fix my feathers? Fix them just like Emma's."

"Okay," said Paul, and he got right to work. "There," said Paul when he was finished. "All done."

Fran looked at herself in the mirror. "Lovely," she said.

"Say," said Paul, "would you like me to paint your nails? I have a special today."

"Oh, yes," replied Fran.

"What color?" asked Paul.

"Pink, I think," said Fran. "No, blue. No, yellow. No, wait, green. No, pink, I think."

Paul painted two of Fran's toes pink, and two blue, and two green.

"Thank you very much, Paul," Fran said.

She hoped she would be the most beautiful chicken at the chicken dance.

On Tuesday Fran ran into Emma near the library.

Emma looked at Fran. "How nice you look today," she said.

"Why, thank you," replied Fran. "I went to Paul's House of Feathers. Paul fixed my feathers and painted my nails. He had a special."

"Painted your nails?" asked Emma. "I have to run. 'Bye, Fran."

Emma ran down the street, straight to Paul's House of Feathers.

"Please, Paul," said Emma, "will you paint my nails?"

"Okay," said Paul.

"I want my left foot purple and my right foot orange," said Emma.

Paul got right to work. "There," he said when he was finished. "All done."

Emma looked at herself in the mirror. "Lovely," she exclaimed. "Any specials, Paul?"

"Not today," he said.

"Too bad," replied Emma.

Emma left the House of Feathers and walked down the street. She needed something more for the chicken dance.

She passed a pet store, a book store, a grocery store, and a dry cleaner. She passed Sadie's Finery Shop. She stopped. Then she went back.

There in Sadie's window was just what Emma needed—a long, fluffy purple feather boa.

"Ooh," said Emma. "Perfect!"

Emma rushed into Sadie's and bought the boa. She wound it around her neck and walked home. She hoped she would be the most beautiful chicken at the chicken dance.

On Wednesday Fran ran into Emma near the bakery.

"Well," said Fran, "that's a nice boa—I guess."

"Thank you," said Emma proudly. "I got it at Sadie's Finery Shop."

"Sadie's?" asked Fran. "See you tomorrow. 'Bye, Emma."

Fran raced down the street to Sadie's. She bought a sparkly gold
boa and wound it around her neck. She was almost ready to leave
when she saw some hats. Fran had never seen so many pretty hats.
"They're on sale," said Sadie. "Would you like to try some on?"
"Why, yes. I believe I would," replied Fran.

SALE
HATS

Fran tried on a hat with ribbons on it. She tried on a hat with birds on it. Then she tried on a hat with fruit all over it.

"I'll take it!" she cried.

She knew she would be the most beautiful chicken at the chicken dance.

On Thursday Fran put on her new hat and boa and went downtown. She ran into Emma near the shoe store.

Emma looked at Fran for a long time. She did not say one word.

"Sadie was having a sale," Fran explained.

Emma nodded. "See you tomorrow," she said.

Emma walked slowly to Sadie's Finery Shop. She was running out of money. But she had enough to buy a little hat with butterflies on it.

"Do you want anything else?" asked Sadie.

Emma looked at some scarves. She looked at the fancy gloves. She looked at the jewelry. But she had no money left.

"No, thank you," she said to Sadie.

The next day was Friday. Fran spent all day getting ready for the chicken dance. So did Emma. Fran fluffed up her feathers. Emma tied bows on her wings. Fran found a pair of pretty pink shoes. Emma put on two bracelets and six long necklaces. Then they both put on their hats and boas.

Fran and Emma met near the supermarket and walked proudly through town. They knew they would be the most beautiful chickens at the chicken dance.

No one else at the dance was dressed the way Fran and Emma were. They felt very special.

"May I have this dance?" Jim asked Fran.

"Of course," said Fran.

Jim and Fran danced around the room. They danced until Jim tripped over Fran's boa and fell down with a loud *ker-thump*!

"I'm sorry!" Fran exclaimed.

"May I have this dance?" Henry asked Emma.

"Of course," said Emma.

Henry and Emma danced around the room. They danced until Henry got his feathers tangled up in Emma's necklaces.

"Ouch!" cried Henry.

"Oh, I beg your pardon!" exclaimed Emma.

Fran and Emma sat down to rest. Fran's shoes were hurting her feet. Emma's hat was falling in her eyes.

"Are you having fun?" Fran asked Emma.

"Not really," said Emma.

"May we have this dance?" asked Fred and Ed.

"I guess so," said Fran.

"I guess so," said Emma.

Fred and Fran and Ed and Emma danced around the room.

As Fran danced three bananas fell off her hat. Then some purple feathers fell off Emma's boa and flew into Ed's eyes.

Fred slipped and fell.

Ed bumped into Mayor Cluck.

"Oh, my goodness!" exclaimed Fran.

"Oh, my goodness!" exclaimed Emma.

As Fred was getting up, Mayor Cluck bumped into him. Fred bumped into Fran. Fran bumped into Emma.

Emma's hat landed in the punch bowl. Fran's boa landed on Mayor Cluck.

Fran gathered up her boa. "We'd better rest a while," she said.
Helen and Ruth walked by. They looked at Fran and Emma. Then
they looked at each other and giggled.

Emma picked her hat out of the punch bowl.

"What's so funny?" she asked.

"Oh, nothing," Helen and Ruth said as they walked away.

"Humph," said Emma. "Let's go, Fran. Helen and Ruth are laughing at us. I think we made a mess of the dance."

Fran and Emma walked back to Emma's house.

"Well," said Emma, "I don't care how beautiful I look. I'm going to take these things off."

"Me, too," said Fran.

After they had taken off their hats, jewelry, bows, and boas, Fran and Emma looked at each other. They looked in the mirror. Fran made a face.

"I think that I'll just put the hat back on. And maybe the boa,"
said Fran.

"And I'll just wear this necklace," said Emma. "And one bracelet.
And maybe the boa."

"But I don't think I'll wear everything at once," said Fran.

"No," said Emma. "Not for a long time."

Fran and Emma smiled at each other.

"Well," said Fran, "I better be going."

"Where are you off to?" asked Emma.

"Why, back to the dance. I'm not going to miss the biggest event in Feather Town. Oh, by the way," said Fran, "tomorrow there will be a sale at Selma's Shoe Store. I think I'll take a look."

"Perhaps," said Emma, "I'll just go along with you."